He was brainy.
He was bouncy.
He was bob-tailed.
He was Brer Rabbit.

And he didn't have many muscles to speak of.

But Rhino and Hippo were always talking about their muscles.

Always boasting about who was stronger, and who was tougher, and who was badder.

"I can lift that mountain with one heave of my horn," Rhino said.

"I can lift that river with one shrug of my shoulder," Hippo said.

"And I can balance a forest on my hip," Rhino said.

"And I can balance this whole island on my nose," Hippo said.

One day Rhino and Hippo were having another bout of boasting when Brer Rabbit stepped in:

"Lifting and balancing is easy to do.
But I can outpull the two of you.
I'm talking tug-o-war, gentlemen."

"Tug-o-what?" Rhino and Hippo asked.

"Tug-o-war," said Brer Rabbit.
"Imagine a long rope.
At one end there's you or you.
At the other end there's me.
We pull and pull to see
who will outpull whom.
Bet my bobtail against your horn.
Bet my whiskers against your waddle.
I'll tire you guys out."

Here we go again, thought Rhino and Hippo.
More hippity-hoppity jokes from the silly rabbit.

But Brer Rabbit was never more serious.

"You think you're the mighty. You think I'm the mite. Well, tomorrow, the mighty will meet the mite in tug-o-war," he declared.

Rhino and Hippo said, "Right." They wanted to get rid of Brer Rabbit and go on with their boasting.

"I can balance the horizon on the tip of my horn," Rhino said.

"I can balance the Milky Way on the tip of my tongue," Hippo said.

"And I can lift the lightning with my left leg," Rhino said.

"And I can lift the thunder with my big toe," Hippo said.

Bright and early the next morning Brer Rabbit returned with a long rope tied around his waist.

The rope went swish-swish-swish through the thick grass and dawdled behind him like an eternal tail.

And though he was struggling with the rope
he shouted in a loud voice for all to hear:
"Wonderful day for tug-o-war to begin.
I'm going to pull that Hippo out of his skin."

Hippo was sniffing the swampy morning
when Brer Rabbit showed up with his rope.

"Here, Hippo," said Brer Rabbit. "Take this end.
I'm off to the far side of the island. Hold tight.
Wait till you feel me pull.
Then start pulling with all your might."

What Hippo didn't know was that Brer Rabbit had planned to meet Rhino on the far side of the island.

"Without a heave or a huff,
I'll pull that Rhino till he's puffed,"
called Brer Rabbit into the empty sky.

When Brer Rabbit got there,
Rhino was already waiting.

"Sorry to be late," Brer Rabbit said.
"A rope takes its time."
And he repeated word for word
what he had told Hippo:

"Here, Rhino, take this end.
I'm off to the far side of the island.
Hold tight. Wait till you feel me pull.
Then start pulling with all your might."

With a bob and a strut Brer Rabbit disappeared into the bushes.

He gave the rope a quick pull on both sides.

This was the moment Rhino and Hippo had been waiting for, yet it seemed to take them by surprise.

Neither Rhino nor Hippo was prepared for such a tugging. Rhino had to use his horn to stop himself from slipping.

Hippo had to dig in his heels to stop himself from sliding.

They pulled and pulled until they were both falling backwards.

Rhino pulling Hippo, Hippo pulling Rhino, and neither had a clue who was pulling whom.

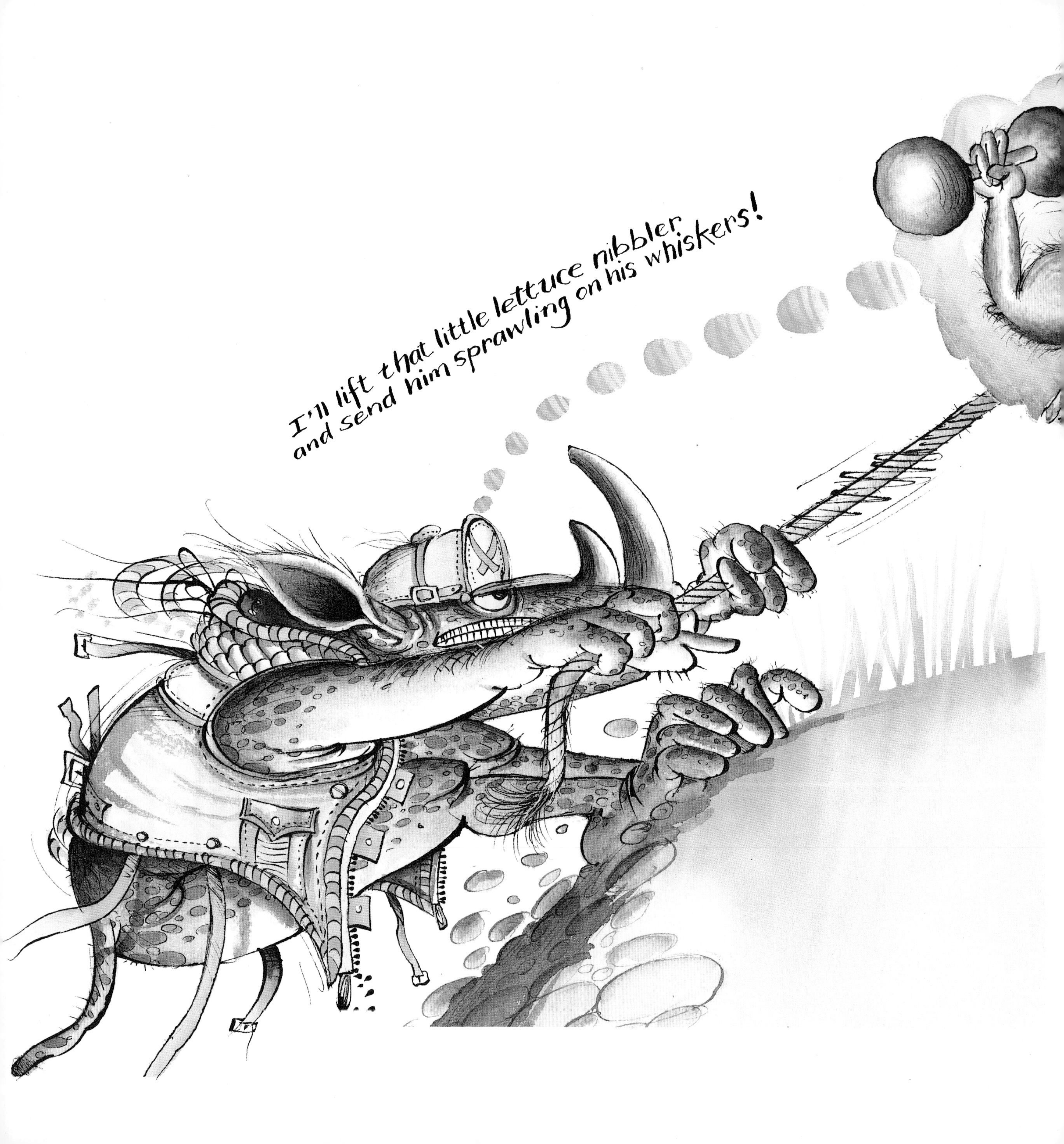
I'll lift that little lettuce nibbler
and send him sprawling on his whiskers!

Maybe this Brer Rabbit was stronger than they thought.

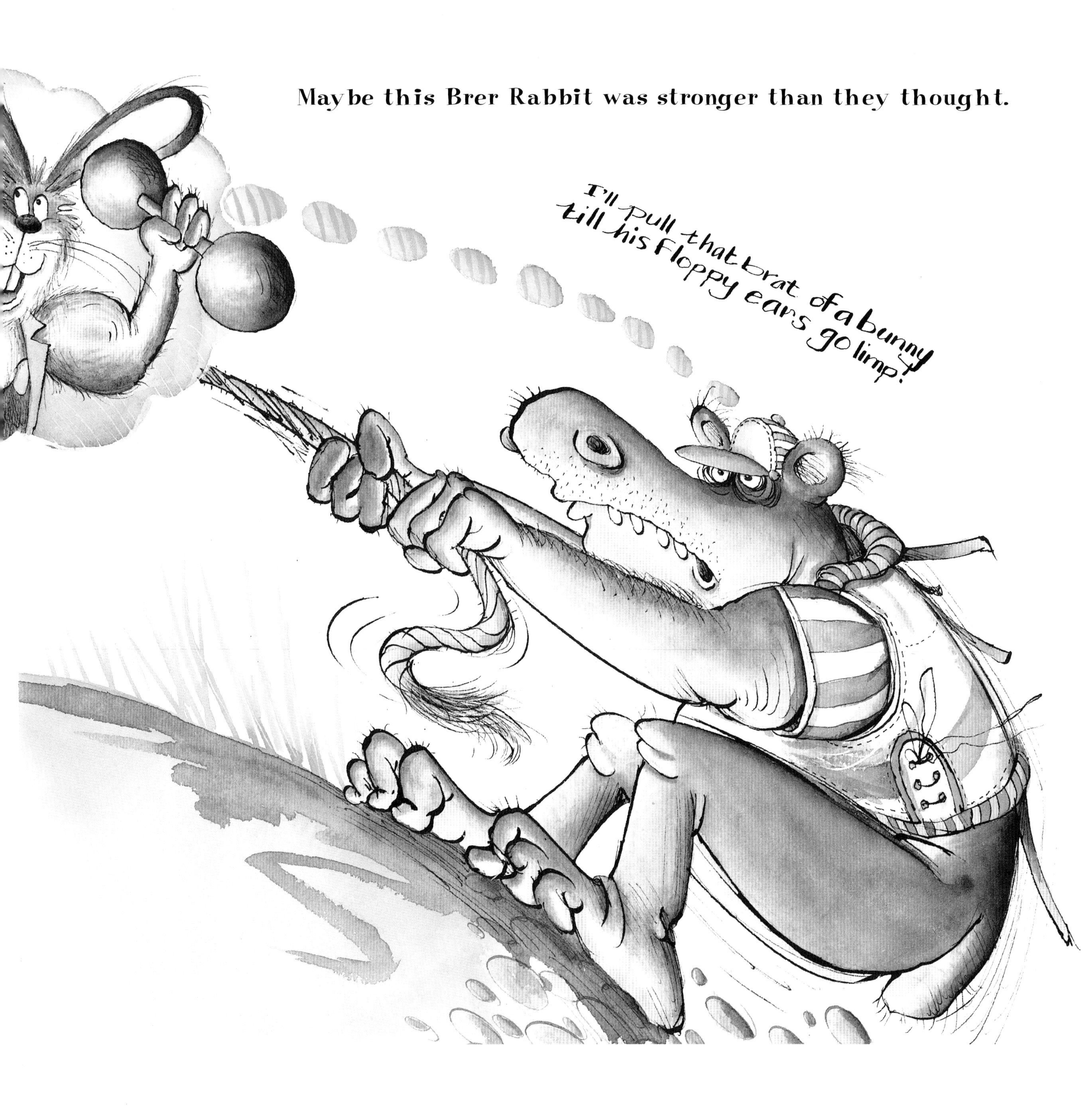

Suddenly, the rope broke in the twinkling of a snap. And Rhino and Hippo fell into the swamp with a mighty splash.

All the monkeys and all the birds - who Brer Rabbit called his friends in high places - were laughing from their tree-top seats.

Among the bushes, Brer Rabbit was cracking up, till he tweaked and twitched all over.

Rhino and Hippo had to laugh.
They knew they had been tricked.
Rhino felt like a fool, and Hippo
felt like a dope.

But from that day on they became friends.
And Brer Rabbit would remind them that

'Friendship is longer than rope.'